THE
BIG
BEYOND

THE STORY OF SPACE TRAVEL

James Carter

Illustrated by Aaron Cushley

Once upon a rocket

a countdown has begun

from 10, 9, 8

to 7 and 6

to 5, 4, 3, 2, 1

Space Shuttle
CHALLENGER

As early people watched the sky
they wished for wings so they could fly.

They dreamt up questions thick and fast...

How **deep** is **space**?

How **far** are **stars**?

Does planet **Mars** have **life** like ours?

And in those stars across the night
they drew some creatures formed of light

from CRAB

to LION

BULL

to BEAR

such starry beasts
were everywhere.

Through telescopes

we found such things

as planets with their

moons and rings.

We learnt we're of the Milky Way

that stars are all so far away

the force of space is gravity

and there are endless galaxies.

GALILEO
GALILEI

Yet still, to fly

was our great aim...

with **kites**

balloons

planes.

and gliders

And then in 1957
rockets soared
towards the heavens.

Through the clouds
up UP and on
out into...

THE
BIG
BEYOND!

SPUTNIK

UP! we sent beyond the night, to orbit Earth, a satellite.

UP! went creatures

LAIKA

dogs

and cats

FELIX

monkeys, turtles, flies and rats.

UP!

in time went

astronauts

space explorers

cosmonauts.

Then summer 1969

what a time for humankind!

A rocket known as **Saturn Five**

with smoke and flames burst into life.

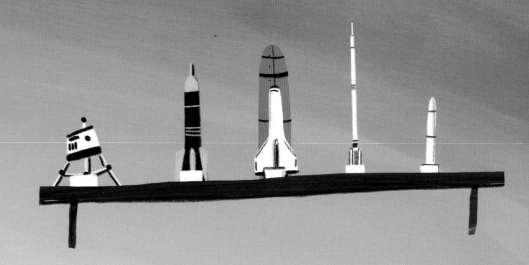

And now in front of their TVs

the whole world watched excitedly.

What great adventure happened next?

Upon the **Moon** two men took **steps!**

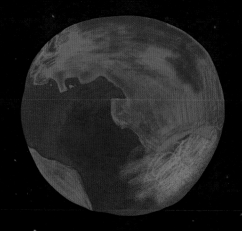

And on that world so strange, so new
they left a **flag**
some **footprints** too.

NEIL
ARMSTRONG

BUZZ
ALDRIN

Since then we've been

UP many times

we've walked in space

launched **satellites**.

And to the planets

spacecraft roam

sending information

home.

To Mars our neighbour

we've sent more –

probes with which

we could explore.

Crafts to land

to test the air

to sample soil

to check what's there.

INTERNATIONAL
SPACE
STATION

New **rockets, rockets** every year will head out through the atmosphere.

We'll need an **astronaut** (or two)

so what do you think?

Could it be YOU?

LET'S LOOK INTO...

Rockets were invented in China in the 13th century, after the Chinese people had discovered how to create gunpowder.

Over the years, rockets have been used as both fireworks and weapons, and since the 1950s, as space-bound craft.

Cosmonaut Yuri Gagarin was the first person to reach space in 1961, in the Russian rocket Vostok 1.

Know how many space travellers there have been so far? Over 500! And more than 200 of these have visited the International Space Station.

Even animals have been sent into space, as humans didn't initially want to risk the dangers. The most well-known is Laika, a Russian stray dog who went into orbit in the spacecraft Sputnik 2 in 1957.

The first astronauts to walk on the Moon were Edwin 'Buzz' Aldrin and Neil Armstrong in 1969. Armstrong's famous words on leaving the craft were, "That's one small step for man, one giant leap for mankind."

Soon there will be tourist trips into space, but you'd better start saving, stargazers – the cost is sky high!

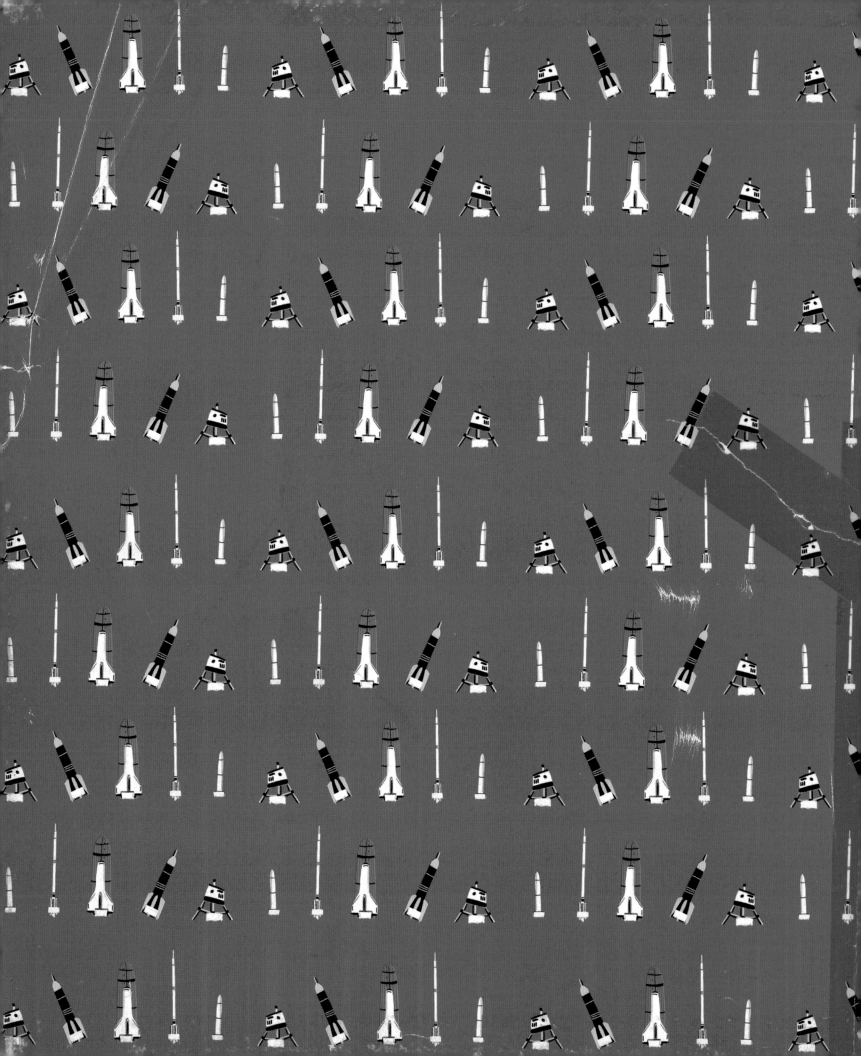